Your Skeleton is Showing

Rhymes of Blunder From Six Feet Under

Written by **Kurt Cyrus**

Illustrated by **Crab Scrambly**

Disney • HYPERION BOOKS

NEW YORK

The folks within these graves and urns
are there because of Michael Stearns
—K. C.

For Charel, who always inspires
—C. S.

Text copyright © 2013 by Kurt Cyrus
Illustrations copyright © 2013 by Crab Scrambly

For information address Disney·Hyperion Books, 114 Fifth Avenue, New York, New York 10011-5690.
First Edition • 10 9 8 7 6 5 4 3 2 1 • H106-9333-5-13105.
Printed in Malaysia
Library of Congress Cataloging-in-Publication Data
Cyrus, Kurt.
Your skeleton is showing : rhymes of blunder from six feet under / by Kurt Cyrus ; illustrated by Crab Scrambly.—1st ed.
p. cm.
ISBN 978-1-4231-3846-4
1. Cemeteries—Juvenile poetry. 2. Dead—Juvenile poetry. I. Scrambly, Crab. II. Title.
PS3553.Y49Y68 2012   811'.54—dc22   2011014439
Reinforced binding
Visit www.disneyhyperionbooks.com

Dog

In a graveyard, through the fog,

I thought I saw a ghostly dog.

He followed me from stone to stone.

The dog was lost. Afraid. Alone.

And also dead. It's plain to see

I couldn't take him home with me.

And so we ventured through the gloom

to try to find his master's tomb.

Tim Limber

"Choked on his elbow," the coroner swore.
Another poor thumb-sucker, greedy for more.

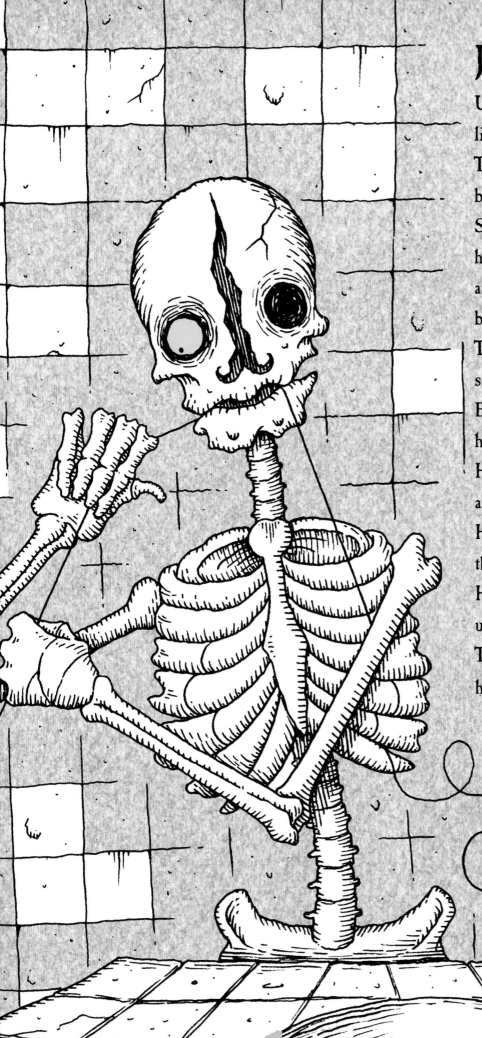

Joe Shmif

Underneath this wilted wreath
lies a guy who has no teeth.
They all were lost, or yanked and tossed,
because the fool had never flossed.
So every night, to make it right,
his bones turn on the bathroom light
and take great care to floss the air
between the teeth that are not there.
The floss goes in, then out his chin,
scraping clean his toothless grin.
But wait—there's more. He can't ignore
his gnarly ribs, all twenty-four.
He takes the twine and puts a shine
all up and down his knobby spine.
High and low, from head to toe,
the frenzied floss goes to and fro.
He isn't done, this skeleton,
until the rising of the sun.
Then back beneath the wilted wreath
he goes to doze, and dream of teeth.

Freddie Diggs

Freddie picked his nose and now he's dead, dead, dead.

He picked and picked and picked until it bled, bled, bled.

His mama came and called his name: "Fred! Fred! Fred!"

But Freddie picked his nose and now he's dead, dead, dead.

FREDDIE DIGGS

Mortimer Poe

When Mortimer Poe was eleven or so,
a gaggle of geese took him down.
Only eleven, and hoisted to heaven
garbed in a goose-feather gown!

Now little Mortie has thirty or forty
panicky geese on the fly.
They flap through the air on a wing and a prayer,
pursued by a vengeful guy—

Mortie, king of the sky!

MORTIMER POE

High-Wire Pete

High-Wire Pete had magic feet
that danced across the rope.
You'd think, in turn, his hands would learn
to tie a knot.

Nope.

Mary Lou South

Mary Lou South had milk in her mouth
when somebody told her a joke.
Catastrophe followed. Before she could swallow,
she sniggered and started to choke.

Up the milk rose. It blew from her nose.
It shot from her ears and her eyes.
How frightful. How scary! That mouthful of dairy
sealed poor Mary's demise.

Everyone blows past their ears and nose.
But *never* blow pasteurize.

Wanda Gripp

Wanda was a hugger.
It's how she said hello.
The folks she squeezed were less than pleased
at how the hugs would go.

She held each victim tightly,
compressed each torso snugly.
Her steel embrace could turn your face
a dozen shades of ugly.

She hugged her friends and neighbors.
Their cats and doggies too.
She pressed their lungs and popped their tongues
and left them black-and-blue.

The crushing now has ended.
Let's give a cheer for Wanda!
Though clearly nuts, it did take guts
to hug an anaconda. . . .

Michael Gann

Michael Gann, the garbage man,
was buried in a garbage can.
No offense was meant to Michael;
some things simply don't recycle.

Ophelia Heft

Gravity wasn't Ophelia's friend.

She battled its hold to the bitter end.

But after she passed, on that beautiful day,

she found herself spinning,

goofing and grinning,

bumping and bouncing and bobbing away.

Crusty Dan

Beneath this stone lies no one.
Its owner, Crusty Dan,
decided not to use this plot.
He's got a better plan.

He plans to be a fossil.
He's waiting for a flood
to carry him and bury him
beneath a sea of mud.

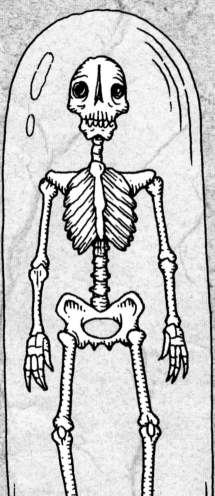

He'll make a big impression.
His fat will melt away,
and every bone will turn to stone.
They'll dig him out someday.

He'll lie in a museum
and there he will remain,
a resident. A *monument*!
The king of his domain!

If only it would rain.

Jumping Jack Barkley

Barkley, the gym teacher, every so often
delivers a pep talk from inside his coffin.
He barks out his favorite fitness tips:
"Wiggle your ears! Now smack your lips!
Now stick out your tongue! Now cross your eyes!
Not *one* of you gets enough exercise!"

Dog

He brought a stick—this dog, the ghost—
for play is what he missed the most.
The stick fell through my open hand.
It wasn't real, you understand.
I tried to pick it up. But no,
a ghostly stick I could not throw.
A solid stick *he* could not catch.

The dog and I were not a match.
And so we ventured, as before,
to read the stones and search some more.

Mrs. Fibble

Every sickness known to science,
Mrs. Fibble got.
From common colds to mumps and molds
to booger blister rot;
scurvy, shingles, tummy tingles,
Picklebee's Complaint . . .
every bug that ever was,
plus quite a few that ain't.

Her patient chart weighed half a ton.
It fell onto her head,
and at the age of ninety-one,
Mrs. F. was dead.

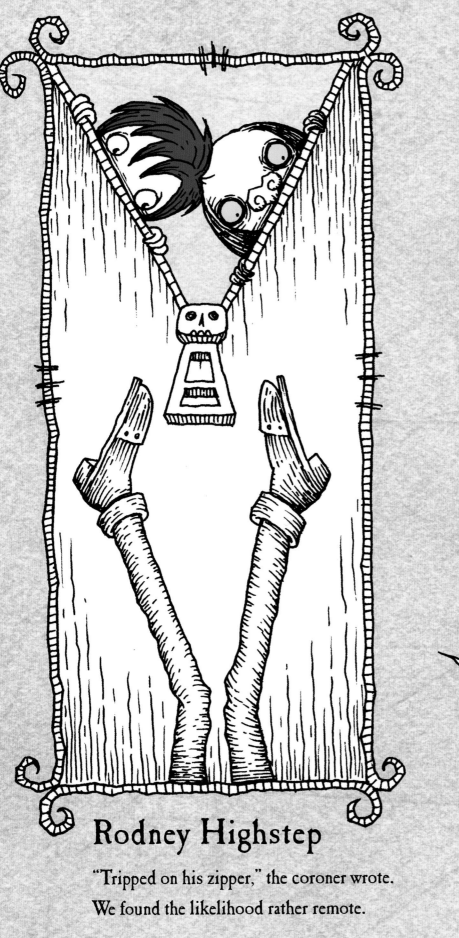

Rodney Highstep

"Tripped on his zipper," the coroner wrote.
We found the likelihood rather remote.

Lem Tremolo

Once upon a podium
a public speaker died
from sweating so much sodium
he shriveled up inside.

Terror frozen on his face,
body fluids leaking.
Just another routine case
of death by public speaking.

Baxter Blink

Baxter Blink blew a stink.
He didn't mean to do it.
The guy was cool. The guy was hip.
He *never* made a social slip,
and then one day he let 'er rip,
and everybody knew it.
When Baxter Blink blew that stink
he really, *really* blew it.

Baxter Blink. Expired. Spent.
Died of deep embarrassment.

Lulu Kaduba

Lulu Kaduba was tuning her tuba
the morning the meteor hit.
It flattened her head. She blew a loud *Blatt!*
The bandleader said: "Kaduba, you're flat."
But nobody there saw the humor in that,
and soon he was forced to quit.
When meteors land in the midst of a band,
it's better to button your wit.

Birdie Duncan

The moment Birdie Duncan died
her ghost was scattered far and wide.
The spooky pieces all lit out
to do the things they'd dreamed about.

First away were Birdie's feet,
skipping barefoot down the street.

Word came in of ghostly hands
thumbing rides to distant lands.

Birdie's beaming face was seen
on every television screen.

One appendage didn't roam:
Birdie's bottom stayed at home.
For a butt there's nothing finer
than a comfy old recliner.

Unknown

Hoofprints. Feathers. Piles of dung!
Who is laid below?
Mysterious letters mark the stone:
EIEIO.

Stubby Flub

Strike the drum and ring the bell
for Stubby Flub, who tripped and fell.
There isn't very much to tell.

He wore his pants extremely low,
and as he waddled to and fro
he flapped and flopped and stubbed his toe.

A wind came up—a northern gale.
His trousers billowed like a sail
and whipped him over, head-to-tail.

Into a Dumpster Stubby fell.
He struck a drum. It rang his bell.
There isn't any more to tell.

Mrs. McBride

Nobody misses you, Mrs. McBride.
You cheated. You lied. You stole.
Even your dog doesn't care that you died;
in fact, she helped dig the hole.

The hole that you're buried in, Mrs. McBride.
The hole where you presently sleep.
She dug it with eagerness, dug it with pride;
dug it exceedingly deep.

Sue Rollenberger

Sue went shopping for some stuff
and rode the escalator.
She didn't step off fast enough.
It grabbed her feet and ate her.

Her mama always used to say,
"Sue, the stairs are safer."
But Sue rode up the lazy way
and rolled back down a wafer.

Bud Pugsley

The coroner ruled:
"Suffocation by hat."
Bud was a lowbrow,
no doubt about that.

Homer O. Goobergomer

Homer Omer Goobergomer never got it going.

He learned to crawl but that was all, and then he started slowing.

He lay around until he found his skeleton was showing.

Lazybones.

Lazybones.

Going . . .

Going . . .

Going . . .

McBuck Buck

Everyone cried when McBuck Buck died.
They just couldn't swallow their sobs.
Their eyes ran like hoses. They blew from their noses
all manner of goobery gobs.

More than a little saliva and spittle,
with stringers and bubbles and such,
merged in a pool of community drool,
everyone cried so much. So much!
Everyone cried so much.

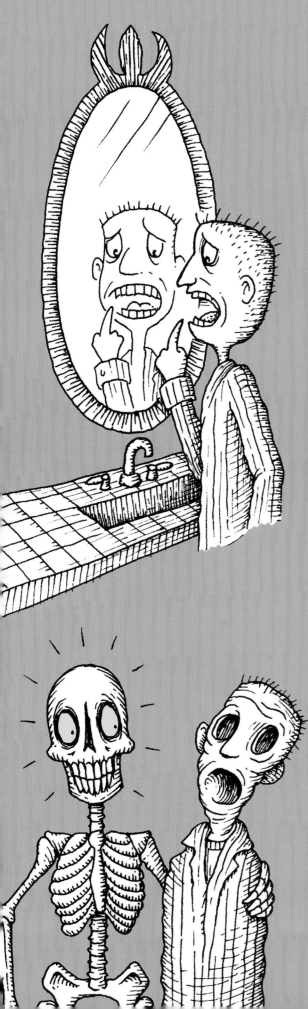

Mo Gringott

Mo had a mirror.
He gave it a grin,
then yelped: "There's a skeleton
under my skin!

"I saw its big teeth,
all bony and bare!
Oh God, what's a skeleton
doing in there?"

Grabbing his teeth,
he tried to pull free.
"Ged oud! Ged oud! Stoff
hiding id vee!"

Out popped the skeleton,
grinning that grin.
"I'm free! I'm free of that
horrible skin!"

Isn't it wonderful?
Both sides win.

Ophelia Heft

"Howdy, my dear," said a voice overhead—
"Howdy! Hey, Howdy!"
"Hello there," I said.

"Hey," said Ophelia. "My sweet little pup.
Howdy, my sugarplum! Up, Howdy! Up!"
Then Howdy, the ghost dog, was no longer there.
He'd sprung like an acrobat into the air.
Together they wobbled around in the mist
as one of them wagged and the two of them kissed.
And then, in the glimmer of dawn . . .

they were gone.

At last the sun broke through the fog,
and there she was. Another dog.
She followed me from stone to stone.
The dog was lost. Afraid. Alone.
And so alive! It's plain to see,
I had to take her home with me.

Another day, another friend,
a new beginning—

and
The End.